Dear Parents,

Psalty on Safari focuses on our Christian responsibility to respond to the needs in the world around us. It illustrates that God desires to develop a sensitive and caring heart in each of us. Through a firsthand trip to a mission hospital in Africa, Psalty the Singing Songbook teaches us to have compassion for others and to care less about our own selfish desires, because God gives us more than we can ever give away.

As with all Psalty products, for this new adventure story, we've chosen struggles and concepts that affect everyone trying to live their Christian faith. We believe that if you learn these concepts as a child, they will stay with you throughout your adult years. And you will be better equipped to live a joyous life, committed to Christ.

Now snuggle close to your little one and follow Psalty; his wife, Psaltina; their booklets Rhythm, Melody, and Harmony; and their trusty dog Blooper on their safari adventure in Africa.

Ernie Rettino and Debby Kerner Rettino

PSALTY ON SAFARI

Scripture quotations are from the *International Children's Bible, New Century Version*. Copyright © 1983, 1986, 1988 by Word Publishing.

Library of Congress Cataloging-in-Publication Data

Rettino, Ernie, 1949-
    Psalty on safari / Ernie Rettino and Debby Kerner Rettino ; design and illustration by Dale Wehlacz.
        p.   cm.
    "Word kids!"
    Summary : After she wins $10.000 and an African safari on a game show. Melody sees firsthand the extreme need in Africa and decides to donate her cash to the missionary work being done there.
    ISBN 0-8499-0896-5
    [1. Christian life—Fiction.   2. Missionaries—Fiction.
3. Africa—Fiction. 4. Books—Fiction.]   I. Rettino, Debby Kerner, 1951-   . II. Wehlacz, Dale, 1960-   ill. III. Title.
PZ7.R32553P5   1991
[E]—dc20
                                        91-500
                                        CIP
                                        AC

Printed in the United States of America

1 2 3 4 9 RRD 9 8 7 6 5 4 3 2 1

PSALTY ON SAFARI

Characters and Story by
Ernie Rettino and Debby Kerner Rettino

Design and Illustration by
Dale Wehlacz

428

WORD *kids!*

WORD PUBLISHING
Dallas · London · Vancouver · Melbourne

"Welcome to 'The Zany Race Against the Clock,'" said host Zany Zach. "Our contestants* today are Psalty the Singing Songbook; his wife, Psaltina; and their booklets, Harmony, Melody, and Rhythm. Also with them is their trusty dog, Blooper."

"Who from your family will answer the questions and run the race?" asked Zany Zach.

"My booklet Melody," answered Psalty proudly.

"Step right up here, Melody," directed Zany Zach. "Answer three questions correctly, and you'll have a chance at the obstacle course*. Now here is your first question: What color is a red pepper?"

"Red!" answered Melody.

"Correct! What fruit did Johnny Appleseed plant?" asked Zany Zach.

"Apples!" said Melody.

"Correct! What language do the French speak?"

"French!" exclaimed Melody.

"Correct!" said Zany Zach. "You just won a chance at the Gooey Sundae Obstacle Course."

"If you finish the course in less than three minutes, you win the grand prize!" Everyone cheered!

"Ready, set, GO!" shouted Zany Zach.

Melody swam through gooey chocolate pudding and raced up a ladder covered with butterscotch sauce. It was hard to hang on! Then she braved buckets of icky blueberry jam as she swung from ring to ring. Only one minute was left on the clock. Slipping and sliding, she crawled through the tumbling whipped cream machine.

Next came the slide of marshmallow goo. Tick, tock, tick, tock — time was running out.

Melody landed "kersplat!" in crushed nuts. She grabbed the cherry and put it on her head. Everybody laughed because she looked just like a chocolate sundae. She ran across the finish line just before the clock buzzed.

"Congratulations, Melody!" said Zany Zach. "You have won the grand prize of ten thousand dollars! And that's not all. You've won a safari* in Africa for you and your family!"

"Wow! Ten thousand dollars!" exclaimed Melody.

"We're going on a safari! Yippee!" shouted Rhythm and Harmony.

Melody cleaned off the icky goo, then joined her family. "A safari sure sounds like fun. But I can't wait to spend my money! I'm gonna buy lots of new things — video games, candy . . ."

"Slow down, Melody," said Psalty. "Aren't you going to give some of your money to the Lord's work?"

"Why? This is my money. I won it," answered Melody.

"Yes," agreed Psalty. "But when we give part of our money to the Lord, it goes where it's REALLY needed. And God gives back to us much more than we can ever give away."

"Well, maybe. But I don't see why I can't keep it all!" pouted Melody.

"I've got a friend who is a missionary* doctor in Africa. Maybe we can see him while we are there," said Psalty.

"Let's go home and start packing!" said Psaltina.

"Maybe I can get some really neat things with my money in Africa!" exclaimed Melody.

When they reached Kenya, a country in Africa, a man with a wide smile met them. "I am your safari guide, George. This way to my van, please."

"Wait a minute," said Melody. "First, I want to buy something with my money."

"Not now, Melody," said Psaltina. "We have to go." Blooper pulled Melody toward the van.

Psalty's family piled into George's van. Off they went to Aberdare National Park*. They passed Masai* men herding cattle. Psalty and the booklets waved at them. The Masais waved back.

As Psalty's family drove along, they spotted many different animals. Hippos bathing in mudholes wiggled their ears. Zebra families ran gracefully across the open plains. Rhythm took lots of pictures from the van window.

George showed them an elephant family playfully splashing each other at their watering hole.

"R - r - r - o - a - r," said the daddy lion as he watched over his pride*. The little lion cubs chased each other's tails as their mother snoozed nearby.

They spent the whole day watching the interesting animals. That night Psalty's family set up tents to sleep in. Before bedtime they told stories and sang songs around the campfire. Through the starry night they could see curious eyes watching them from the bushes.

The next day they saw an animal with spots and a long neck. "It's a baby giraffe," said Melody.

"Where are its mother and father?" Rhythm asked.

"I don't know," George answered. "It looks like he has a broken leg. His parents must have gone off and left him."

"He looks hungry. He's too little to take care of himself. Can we help him, George?" pleaded Melody.

"There is a missionary hospital not too far away. We can take him there. But getting him into the van is going to be a hard job!" answered George.

The booklets picked some tender, green leaves for the hungry little giraffe. Psalty, Psaltina, George, and Blooper helped herd the limping giraffe into the van.

They had to open the sunroof for the giraffe's long neck to stick through.

Soon they drove through the gate of the missionary hospital. A doctor came out to meet them.

"It's my old friend, Dr. Marosi," said Psalty.

"Psalty the Singing Songbook, what a surprise!" said Dr. Marosi as he shook Psalty's hand. "What brings you here?"

"My booklet Melody won a trip to Africa on a TV game show."

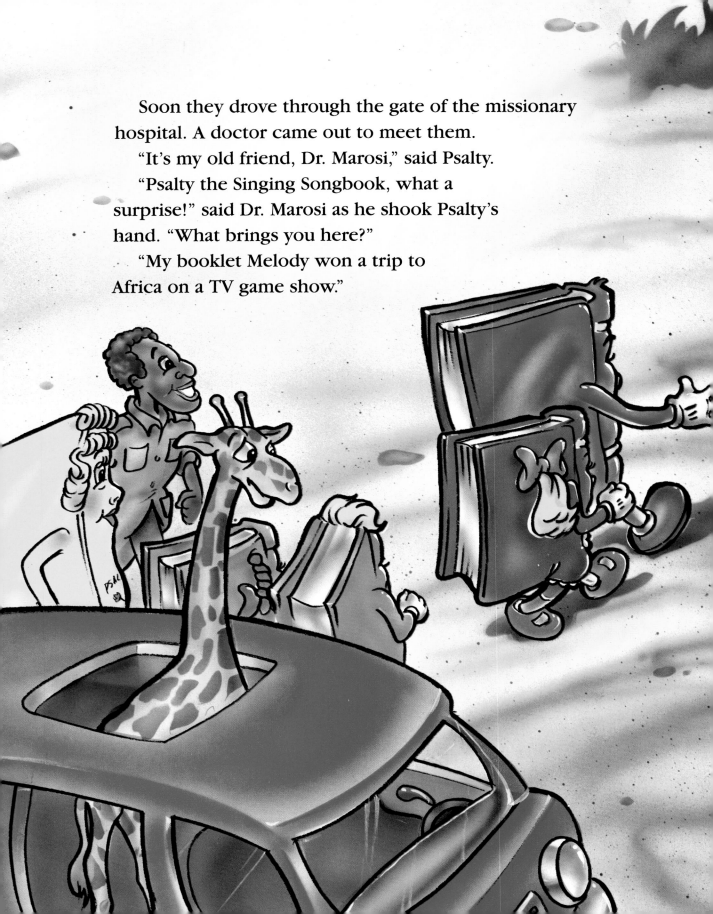

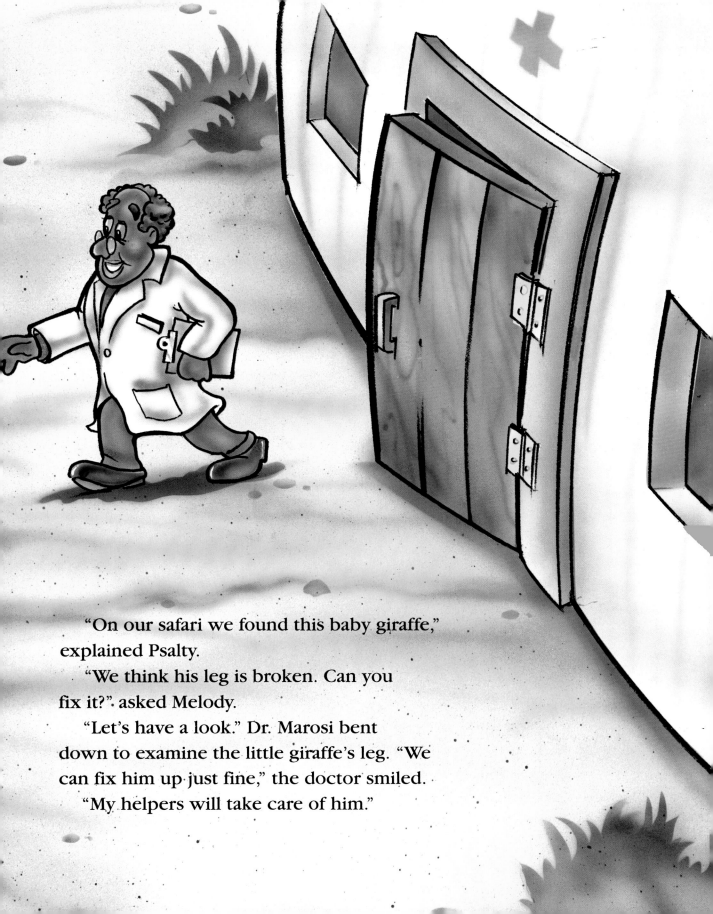

"On our safari we found this baby giraffe," explained Psalty.

"We think his leg is broken. Can you fix it?" asked Melody.

"Let's have a look." Dr. Marosi bent down to examine the little giraffe's leg. "We can fix him up just fine," the doctor smiled.

"My helpers will take care of him."

"Would you like to see the hospital?" asked Dr. Marosi.
"That would be great," agreed Psalty's family.

Dr. Marosi took them to see everything. They saw where the doctors and nurses worked and the rooms where the patients slept. There were lots of beds with children in them. "Why are there so many sick children, Dr. Marosi?" asked Melody.

"They drank bad water, and it made them sick," answered the doctor sadly.

"Why don't they drink fresh water?" asked Harmony.

"It has been very dry where they live. A lot of the fresh water has dried up."

"They need new wells that pump fresh water so they will not get sick. We help them as much as we can. But we don't have the money to dig enough wells," said Dr. Marosi.

Melody walked over to a little girl who was hugging a little rag doll. "How are you feeling?" asked Melody.

"Much better now. Dr. Marosi is taking good care of me," answered the little girl. "Are you going to take care of me, too?"

"Maybe I can," answered Melody.

Melody thought about the fun things she was going to buy. Ten thousand dollars would buy a lot of video games and candy. She thought and thought. Then she looked back at the sick little girl and made a decision.

"Dr. Marosi," said Melody, "I also won ten thousand dollars on the game show."

"I was going to spend it on things I didn't even need. But, I've changed my mind. I'd like to give the money to your missionary hospital. You can use it to dig wells and help these children."

"Thank you, Melody. God will bless you for helping others," said Dr. Marosi. He gave Melody a big hug.

"Dad, can we stay here at the Mission Hospital for a while? I'd like to help the sick children. And we need to care for the baby giraffe," said Melody.

"It's okay with me if it's okay with Dr. Marosi," said Psalty.

"That would be great," said the doctor.

"When the little giraffe's leg is healed, I will come back and get all of you," said George. "We will take the giraffe back to where we found him. Then I will take you to the airport."

Psalty and his family waved good-bye to George. Soon they were busy helping at the hospital.

Psaltina helped cook meals. Rhythm and Blooper washed floors. Harmony helped watch over the babies. Psalty sang with the children and made them very happy. Melody took special care of the little girl and the giraffe until they were completely well. Melody's heart was full of love. It was true. God *had* given her more than she could ever give away.

GLOSSARY

Contestants (kən-tes´-tənts) — People who take part in a game or contest.

Obstacle course (ob´-stə-kəl kôrs) — A track that has many things in the way to keep a person from going fast.

Safari (sə-fär´-ē) — A long trip where you see animals in Africa.

Missionary (mish´-ə-ner-ē) — A person sent by a church to do special work for God.

Masai (mə-sī´) — African people who live in the highlands of Kenya. Many of them take care of cattle.

Aberdare (Ab-ər-da(ə)r´)
National Park — A large national park in Kenya where many wild animals are protected.

Pride (prīd) — A group of lions.

THERE'S MORE TO COME! Follow Psalty and family's round-the-world adventures in these other great stories:

PSALTY IN THE SOVIET CIRCUS—a memorized Bible verse brings Psalty comfort when he is mistakenly thrown in jail.

PSALTY IN ALASKA—a snowy dogsled race helps Rhythm learn that we don't have to be afraid of losing if we do our best.

PSALTY IN THE SOUTH PACIFIC—being marooned on a South Seas island shows Harmony how trouble can help us grow.

PSALTY IN EGYPT—a kidnapping in the shadow of the Great Pyramid ends in a lesson about the life-changing power of prayer and God's love.

PSALTY IN AUSTRALIA—a vacation "down under" gives Psalty's family a glimpse of God's amazing creativity and reminds them that God has a unique plan for everyone.